NIGHT IN THE COUNTRY

For Bob Verrone

NIGHT IN THE COUNTRY

story by CYNTHIA RYLANT

pictures by MARY SZILAGYI

Aladdin Books
Macmillan Publishing Company   New York
Collier Macmillan Canada   Toronto
Maxwell Macmillan International Publishing Group
New York   Oxford   Singapore   Sydney

There is no night so dark, so black as night in the country.

In little houses people lie sleeping and dreaming about daytime things, while outside — in the fields, and by the rivers, and deep in the trees — there is only night and nighttime things.

There are owls. Great owls with marble eyes who swoop
among the trees and who are not afraid of night in the country.
Night birds.

There are frogs. Night frogs who sing songs for you every night: *reek reek reek reek.* Night songs.

And if you are one of those people in one of those little houses, and if you cannot sleep, you will hear the sounds of night in the country all around you.

Outside, the dog's chain clinks as he gets up for a drink of water.

Far over the hill you hear someone open and close a creaking screen door. You wonder who is up so late.

And, if you lie very still, you may hear an apple

fall from the tree in the back yard.

Listen:

Pump!

Later, the rabbits will patter into your yard and eat pieces of your fallen apples. But only when they think you are asleep.

And all around you on a night in the country
are the groans and thumps and squeaks that houses
make when they are trying, like you, to sleep.

Outside . . .

A raccoon mother licks her babies.

A cow nuzzles her calf.

An old pig rolls over in the barn.

And toward morning, one small bird will be the first to tell everyone that night in the country is nearly over.

The owls will go to sleep, the frogs will grow quiet, the rabbits will run away.

Then they will spend a day in the country
listening to you.

First Aladdin Books edition 1991   Text copyright © 1986 by Cynthia Rylant. Illustrations copyright © 1986 by Mary Szilagyi. All rights reserved. No part of this book may be reproduced or transmitted in any form or by any means, electronic or mechanical, including photocopying, recording, or by any information storage and retrieval system, without permission in writing from the Publisher.   Aladdin Books   Macmillan Publishing Company   866 Third Avenue New York, NY 10022   Collier Macmillan Canada, Inc.   1200 Eglinton Avenue East, Suite 200 Don Mills, Ontario M3C 3N1   Printed in Hong Kong by South China Printing Co. Ltd.
1 2 3 4 5 6 7 8 9 10
Library of Congress Cataloging-in-Publication Data   Rylant, Cynthia. Night in the country/ story by Cynthia Rylant: pictures by Mary Szilagyi. – 1st Aladdin Books ed. p.   cm. Summary: Text and illustrations describe the sights and sounds of nighttime in the country. [1. Night – Fiction.   2. Country life – Fiction.]   I. Szilagyi, Mary, ill.   II. Title. [PZ7.R982Ni   1991] [E] – dc20   90-1043   CIP   AC

A hardcover edition of *Night in the Country* is available from Bradbury Press, Macmillan Publishing Company.